My thanks to Jean Arbeille

First American Edition published in 2008 by
Enchanted Lion Books, 201 Richards Street, Studio 4, Brooklyn, NY 11231

Originally published in French as **Gustave est un poisson** by Adam Biro Jeunesse © 2004

Translation © 2008 Enchanted Lion Books
Translated by Claudia Bedrick

Series Director: Maylis de Kerangal
Graphic Design: Anne Catherine Boudet
Layout: Fréderic Peyrichou
Assistant: Virginie Gerard-Gaucher

[A CIP record is on file with the Library of Congress]

ISBN-10: 1-59270-101-9
ISBN-13: 978-1-59270-101-8

Printed in China

GUS
IS A FISH

By Claire Babin

Illustrated by Olivier Tallec

ENCHANTED LION BOOKS
New York

Gus plays in his bath surrounded by a family of ducks.
He stretches out just like his mommy does when she
goes swimming on vacation.
"Mommy, look! I'm swimming, I'm swimming!"
"Bravo! You're a real little fish," says mommy.

Gus wants to put his head in the water, but he's a little scared, as usual. Once he's done it, however, he is able to breathe without choking! It's like magic! He slithers between his bath toys, moving cautiously at first, then more and more quickly. The bathtub seems so big now! How easy it is to be a FISH.

A little wave comes and propels Gus into a POND.
He sees WATER LILIES and a FROG. From somewhere
above, a little shadow falls on the water. It's a DRAGONFLY
that darts busily from leaf to leaf.

Rays of sunlight illuminate the middle of the pond like a flashlight. Gus feels the water glide over his SCALES, gentle as a bedtime backrub. As he swims, he passes a CATFISH and a multitude of tiny TADPOLES. He is no longer alone!

Gus swims better and better.
Thanks to his FINS, he can speed up,
jump and dive. It gets easier and easier.
Fascinated by the little bubbles dancing
in front of him, he chases them for fun.

From the corner of his eye, Gus spies two webbed feet moving together. He swims along with them: one, two, one, two. A DUCKLING plunges its head into the water and looks at Gus with surprise. The two swim together side-by-side across the pond.

Having arrived at a forest of REEDS, Gus
and the duckling play a lively game of
hide-and-seek. After a while, the little duck
tires and returns to its mother on the
BANKS of the pond.

Suddenly, Gus feels as though he's being watched. Whatever is looking at him advances very quietly. It's an enormous fish that charges right for him! It's a fierce PIKE with many sharp teeth. Gus turns around and swims away as quickly as possible.

Whew! Gus has gotten away from the pike. He reaches the banks of the pond where willow branches fall gently over the water. He hides among the reeds. Safe, he shivers with relief. He had been so frightened!

Gus is about to swim off again when he hears his mommy calling him. "Gus, please finish your game of fish. It's time to scrub up and get out of the bath." Gus lifts his head up slowly and sees that he's back in the tub, with all his toys and his mommy's smiling face.

Fish and Water Words

 A **POND** is a medium-sized area of stagnant water. Its plant and animal life develop in accordance with the seasons.

 The **WATER LILY** is a plant that lives in water. Its magnificent white, yellow or red flowers and its large floating leaves serve as a resting spot for frogs, insects, and even small birds.

 A **FROG** is an animal that lives in a pond, lake, or fresh-water pool. It moves by hopping and swimming. Though usually green or reddish in color, poisonous varieties can be orange, yellow, or even blue! Frogs croak.

 The **DRAGONFLY** is an insect with four wings. It lives near rivers, ponds and water pools and eats the insects that it captures in flight. Some, called damsels, can be recognized by their wings, which are kept vertical when they rest.

SCALES cover the body of a fish and are distributed over its skin like tiles or shingles over a roof. Their size, shape and color vary according to species.

The **CATFISH** has a rather strange appearance. Its body is long, its skin is bare and slimy, its large head is flattened and its eyes are tiny. Like the cat, it has long whiskers that help it to find its way in the darkness and to sense its prey. Catfish live in rivers, canals and ponds.

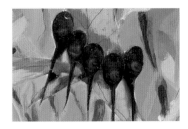

TADPOLES are the babies of frogs, toads and newts. At the beginning of spring, a female frog lays nearly 3,000 eggs, which give birth to as many tadpoles within two-to-three weeks.

FINS allow a fish to swim and move thanks to the muscles in its body. The fin at the end of its tail is the most important since it propels the fish, acting as its motor. The other fins on a fish's body serve to balance it, maintaining equilibrium.

A **DUCKLING** is a young duck. The duck is a bird that leaves the nest and manages to feed itself shortly after hatching. Its feathers change color as it becomes a full-grown duck.

The PIKE, known as the "freshwater shark," is a carnivorous fish. Full-grown pike have a large jaw, hundreds of teeth, and eat mainly fish, some as large as themselves. When a pike detects a fish nearby, it attacks with lightning speed. Pike can reach a length of 6 feet and a weight of 75 pounds. They are typically found in shallow, clear waters that are rich with vegetation.

REEDS – The reed is a plant that grows along the banks of a body of water, often of ponds. Like rushes, reeds form their own miniature forest that shelters and nourishes a number of pond inhabitants, such as fish, ducks and a multitude of insects.

BANKS are the often-steep slopes of land adjoining a river, lake, or pond. Situated at the frontier between two natural worlds (aquatic and terrestrial), banks form an enormously rich environment. Certain birds even nest here.

A **FISH** lives in water. It breathes thanks to its gills, and it moves with the help of its fins. Most often its skin is covered with scales. The shape of its body is linked to its way of life, through which its particular habits develop. Fish with long bodies are good swimmers in rapid water. Flat fish are the weakest swimmers and live near the bottom of a body of water. Still other fish resemble snakes. These move by gliding between rocks and plants along the shore.